THORFIN THE NICEST VIKING

To Holly and Theo Rhodes,

and to all at Durris School and Crossroads Nursery – D.M.

To all the little Vikings – R.M.

Kelpies is an imprint of Floris Books
First published in 2020 by Floris Books

Text © 2020 David MacPhail. Illustrations © 2020 Floris Books
David MacPhail and Richard Morgan have asserted their rights
under the Copyright, Designs and Patent Act 1988 to
be identified as the Author and Illustrator of this Work

The publisher acknowledges subsidy from
Creative Scotland towards the publication
of this volume

 This book is also
available as an eBook

British Library CIP data available
ISBN 978-178250-637-9
Printed and bound by MBM Print SCS Ltd, Glasgow

 Floris Books supports sustainable forest management
by printing this book on materials made from wood that
comes from responsible sources and reclaimed material

MIX
Paper from
responsible sources
FSC® C117931

Thorfinn
and the
Putrid Potion

written by David Macphail
illustrated by Richard Morgan

Young Kelpies

HARALD THE SKULL-SPLITTER
CHIEF OF INDGAR

THORFINN THE
VERY-VERY-NICE-INDEED

RAGWICH THE
SOOTHSAYER

PIEBALD THE
POTION-MAKER

SCOTLAND

KINGDOM OF GALLOWAY

KING FERGUS'S FORT

DUNTRODDIN VILLAGE

INDGAR VILLAGE

NORWAY

THORFINN'S JOURNEY

CHAPTER 1

One brisk autumn day, the villagers of Indgar trudged
home from the fields. Their foreheads glistened with
sweat. Their muscles ached. They were licking their
lips, thinking about all the meaty goodies they were
going to eat, because the harvest was finally in and
it was time for FEASTING. And there was NOTHING the
Vikings loved more than a

HUGE

SLAP-UP

FEAST!

Carrying their pitchforks and scythes over their shoulders, led by Erik the Ear-Masher, a ferocious, one-eyed bear of a man, they tramped into the village square. Only they did NOT find a Viking feast waiting for them, but...

A TEA PARTY.

The whole marketplace was draped with bunting, and tables were covered with crisp white tablecloths. There were fancy place settings, tiered cake stands and platters of teeny-tiny finger sandwiches, plus great mounds of scones with cream and jam. And, in the middle of each table, a steaming pot of pinecone tea, complete with frilly tea cosy.

A small, freckle-faced boy was humming and whistling as he laid out plates, while a speckled pigeon danced along the table behind him, pecking up stray crumbs.

The Vikings gaped in horror.

"THORFINN!" barked Erik the Ear-Masher.

The boy turned, a gentle smile on his face, and doffed his helmet. "Good afternoon, my dear friends. And what a lovely—"

"CORK IT, THORFINN!" boomed Erik. "WHERE. IS. OUR. FOOD!?"

"FOOOOOODDD!" the crowd groaned, sounding like a band of cranky old cave trolls.

Thorfinn gestured towards the tables. "Here it is, my friends. Feast away!"

Erik jabbed his thick, sausagey forefinger at the dainty bits of bread. "What d'you call these minuscule things?"

"Sandwiches," Thorfinn replied cheerily. "You can have smoked crab and lettuce, or salmon and cucumber."

"LETTUCE?" cried Erik. "Vikings don't eat LETTUCE!"

"NO!" roared the crowd.

"Lettuce is for rabbits!" yelled one man.

"Yeah!" another cut in. "It's too, uh... What's the phrase I'm looking for?" He screwed up his face in concentration.

Thorfinn's eyes lit up. "Ooh, I love this game. Do you mean... high in nutrients? Rich in vitamins?"

"Non-meaty?" suggested someone else.

"Yes, that's it! It's too non-meaty!" yelled the man. "We Vikings HATE non-meaty vegetables."

Erik glowered at Thorfinn. "We don't want your pathetic sandwiches and wimpy little scones! WE WANT MEAT!"

He smashed his fist down on a table. The plates, cutlery, cake stands and scones jumped three feet in the air, landing in a disorganised clatter. The crowd bellowed in approval.

Thorfinn and his pet pigeon, Percy, stared at the mess in mild confusion. "Oops! Don't worry, I shall re-set the table in no time at all."

Thorfinn was the village chief's son, which was, quite frankly, the only thing that stopped the crowd from burying him up to his neck in one of the fields and pelting him with rotten cabbages. It didn't matter that he'd saved the village many times over. What mattered was that he was *nice* and *polite*, which were definitely NOT good Viking qualities.

Erik scowled at a small, flame-haired girl wearing a helmet that was far too big for her, who was lounging on a bench, stuffing her face with scones. This was Thorfinn's best friend and anger-management coach, Velda. Her job was to try and make Thorfinn *less* polite and *more* angry, like a real Viking, but she was failing miserably. Her favourite hobby was throwing axes, preferably at her enemies, but she wasn't picky.

"YOU!" barked Erik. "You're supposed to make sure he doesn't do things like this!"

Velda gulped down a mouthful of scone and belched. "BAAARP! I told him. I always tell him, but he never listens."

Erik glared at a thin, wiry old man who was lying across the bench opposite Velda, fast asleep.

ZZZZZZZZZZZ...

This was the village wise man, Oswald.

"And you, you old FART!" Erik kicked the bench. Oswald rolled off and fell face down in a muddy puddle.

The old man didn't even stir. Indeed, he continued to snore, blowing bubbles in the murky water.

ZZZZZZZ... Bbbbbbbbbb...

ZZZZZZZ... Bbbbbbbbbb...

But before Erik could wake him, an eerie silence suddenly fell over the marketplace. A dark shadow appeared, bearing down on the villagers.

Though BEAR-ing is probably not the right word. It was more like CHICKEN-ing, because staring down at them was the face of a massive goggly-eyed CHICKEN.

CHAPTER 2

The chicken, as it turned out, was NOT a live chicken, but a huge headdress made out of a dead one, complete with splayed wings and legs dangling either side of the wearer's face.

The wearer was a tall, skinny man with a shock of wild black hair and wide, staring eyes. As goggly, in fact, as the eyes of the stuffed chicken on his head. He wore a bearskin cloak but was bare-chested, except for a large silver medallion hanging from a chain. He was also covered in strange tattoos.

Looming over the crowd from a nearby roof, the
man bellowed:

"WOOOGAHHHH!"

After a moment of stunned silence, Erik the Ear-Masher gasped. "Ragwich!?"

The villagers erupted in cheers. "HUZZAH! Ragwich is back!"

The loud cheers finally woke Oswald, who struggled to his feet, wiping mud from his face. As he eyed the visitor, he made a weary groaning noise, sounding like a budgie taking its last breath before dropping off its perch.

Thorfinn skipped over to his elderly friend. "Pardon me, old bean, but who exactly is Ragwich?"

"A wandering soothsayer," replied Oswald in his whiny, nasal voice. "He *claims* to be able to speak to the gods and predict the future."

"Why is everyone celebrating?" asked Velda.

"Because," said Erik, turning towards them, "Ragwich *always* brings a good harvest."

Thorfinn scratched his head. "Pardon me, dear sir, but the villagers have already brought in the harvest. Isn't he, well, a bit late?"

Erik glared at Thorfinn. "He hasn't visited for several years, and we've had terrible harvests."

Velda snorted. "He probably waited to see what they were like, then decided not to put in an appearance."

"Ragwich wouldn't do that!" hissed Erik.

"Why not? He's got a sneaky look about him," replied Velda. "And I wouldn't trust anyone who wears a dead chicken on their head."

"HOW DARE YOU! It helps him communicate with the gods!" Erik's eye was bulging angrily.

Ragwich jumped from the roof and then gazed down at Thorfinn like he was inspecting a tiny insect. "WHO-OO-OOO is this?"

"He's nobody!" said Erik, trying to push Thorfinn out of the way.

"What d'you mean, NOBODY?!" scowled Velda. "He's the chief's son!"

Erik gritted his teeth. "Don't you dare annoy the soothsayer! If you do, he might leave, and not say any sooths!"

Ragwich suddenly leapt in the air and roared.

"WOOGAH-WOOGAH!"

The villagers fell to their knees, including Erik, who boomed, "SHHHH! HE'S HAVING A VISION!"

They watched in silence as the soothsayer's eyes danced around in their sockets, like flies trapped in a bottle.

"OOGAH-GOOGAH! GOOGAH-HOOGAH! OOGAH-GEEGAH!"

"Pardon me," Thorfinn said, "but what's he saying?"

"SSHHH!" Erik whispered. "Can't you see, he's talking in the old runes!"

Thorfinn's brow creased in an ever-so-polite way. "I hate to point this out, my dear friend, but Oswald has taught me many ancient languages."

Oswald nodded. "That I have, young Thorfinn."

"And that doesn't sound like any of them. In fact, it sounds rather like he's just shouting 'oogah-geegah' over and over again."

"Yeah, and hoping we're stupid enough to be impressed," added Velda loudly.

The crowd gasped in horror. Ragwich pointed a long, bony finger at Thorfinn, fixing him with his googly eyes. "That boy... is a CURSE on this village."

Then the soothsayer shifted his stare to Velda. "And that girl... should be playing with dolls, not AXES."

"Right!" Velda threw down her beloved axe, rolled up her sleeves and cracked her knuckles. "I don't care who he is, he's getting it!"

Oswald grabbed hold of Velda and pulled her back. Meanwhile, Erik's son,

Olaf, who was almost as ugly as his father (but at least five times more stupid, which is *really* saying something), burst through the crowd. "He's right! Thorfinn *is* a curse!"

The villagers roared in agreement, lending Olaf encouragement. "First, he ruins our feast with his daft tea party, and now he shames us by insulting the soothsayer!"

The mob hollered again.

"I vote we dunk him in the village cesspit!" Olaf yelled excitedly.

An enthusiastic chant of "CESSPIT! CESSPIT!" filled the square before the crowd surged forward.

The soothsayer's eyes gleamed with satisfaction.

CHAPTER 3

BLAM!

The doors of the grain store burst open onto the village square. Standing there, heaving giant sacks of grain over each shoulder, was Harald the Skull-Splitter, village chief and Thorfinn's father. He was bigger and more fearsome than any other Viking in all of Norway. So fearsome, in fact, that his enemies did a little wee in their pants at the mere mention of his name.

"What's all this racket?!" he boomed. "I'm trying to tally up our harvest and I can't hear myself count!"

"Thorfinn is embarrassing us, Chief!" yelled Olaf.

Harald dropped his grain sacks, and moved between the villagers and his son. He fixed Olaf with a ferocious glare. "So what?"

Erik stepped forward, his knuckles clenched white upon his sword hilt. "Your boy is making us look like idiots in front of Ragwich. *He* says Thorfinn's a curse on the village!"

The two men butted their heads together like a pair of duelling stags. Harald had an incredibly twitchy eye when he got angry. Wild boars had been known to turn and flee at just one twitch, and now Harald turned it full force on Erik. "My boy has saved this village countless times, and your miserable son's hide with it!"

"Aye, saved us from your stupid mistakes, more like!" retorted Olaf.

Erik snarled. "If I'd been chief there wouldn't have been any stupid mistakes!"

Harald roared, whipped out his axe and brought it crashing down on a wooden bench, smashing it to smithereens. "That'll be your head in a minute!"

Ragwich's eyes glimmered as he watched the two

men growl at each other. He toyed with the sparkly silver medallion hanging round his neck and smirked.

"OOGAH-GEEGAH!" He suddenly thrust out his arms, draping them round the men's shoulders. "It is not your destiny to fight, my friends."

Erik stepped back, loosening his grip on his sword. "If you say so, soothsayer."

Harald glared at Erik a moment longer before his eye stopped twitching. "Fine."

"Why don't we share a cup of my favourite mead?" added Ragwich.

Erik's good eye lit up. "Ooh, mead?"

Harald gave a booming laugh, all his anger forgotten. "I LOVE mead!"

Ragwich turned to his horse, which was just as goggle-eyed as he was, and fished in a saddlebag. He juggled two bottles, one big, one small, as if he were performing a magic trick. Velda eyed him suspiciously as he stuffed the smaller bottle in his trouser pocket. He turned back, presenting the larger bottle to Harald. "There. My favourite mead."

The three men marched off to the Great Hall.

"We'll have something to eat too, a feast! What do you say?" boomed Harald.

"I only eat turnips," said Ragwich.

"REALLY?" asked Harald with disgust.

"The turnip is a sacred vegetable."

"Fine, you eat turnips." Erik slapped the soothsayer on the back. "We'll eat MEAT!"

With the excitement over (and Thorfinn no longer in danger of being dunked in poo), the villagers wandered off to find meat of their own.

"Don't forget the lovely sandwiches and yummy cakes, my dear pals!" Thorfinn called after the crowd.

Velda elbowed him in the ribs. "I'd quit while you're ahead if I were you."

Oswald turned to them. "Do I have mud on me?"

Velda looked him up and down. His face was splattered, his beard was caked, and there were large brown splodges covering the front of his robe.

"Nah," she replied. "You're good."

CHAPTER 4

Thorfinn and his friends made their way to Oswald's house, which was through the forest and up a hill, perched high above a waterfall.

After changing his robe, Oswald brewed up some pinecone tea. Thorfinn sat outside, feeding Percy nuts, while Velda practised with her axe.

"The villagers seem to like Ragwich rather a lot, don't they?" Thorfinn said.

Oswald slurped his tea like a hog drinking from a puddle. "The villagers aren't very clever. They can't see Ragwich for what he is."

"A con man!" shouted Velda. "And he said I should be playing with dolls. Well, I'll show him what I do with dolls!" Velda had 'borrowed' some on the way up to the house and lined them up against a wall. Screaming like a banshee, she spun through the air and threw her axe at them.

Oswald chortled as he watched the dolls explode one by one in a puff of feathery stuffing. "Yes, he *is* a con man. We'll have to keep an eye on—"

Oswald was interrupted by a gigantic **HONK!** coming from the direction of the village.

"What's that noise, old bean?" asked Thorfinn.

"It's the emergency moose," whined Oswald. The villagers kept an old moose tied up in the marketplace – its tail was only to be yanked in emergencies, such as the village running out of ale, or someone finding a stray vegetable in their meaty stew.

"I bet this has something to do with that chicken-wearing trickster!" scowled Velda.

They raced downhill as fast as they could, which

wasn't very fast at all thanks to Oswald. "I can't help it. My bunions are playing up!" he moaned.

As they came out of the trees, a familiar figure bounded towards them, waving his arms.

"Thorfinn! Thorfinn!"

"Oh, it's my good friend, Harek," said Thorfinn.

Thorfinn had his own ship, and his own crew, and Harek the Toe-Stamper was one of them. He was possibly the most accident-prone man in all of Norway, which he now proved by tumbling headlong into a muddy ditch.

SPLATTT!

As they hauled him out, his eyes were pointing in two different directions – though for Harek this was quite normal.

"What's the matter, my friend?" Thorfinn asked.

Harek spat a long stream of ditchwater out of his mouth, then gasped for air. "It's your father, Thorfinn. He's fallen asleep and won't wake up!"

CHAPTER 5

Inside the Great Hall, it was smoky and dim. The only light came from the blazing hearth. Harald lay on a table amid mounds of food, scattered plates and upturned drinking horns. A fur blanket had been draped over him and his bushy beard was spread out like a giant hairy bib. He was snoring peacefully.

ZZZZZZZZ...

Thorfinn patted his father's hands, which were clasped over his great barrel-shaped chest. "Dear old Dad. I do hope he wakes up soon." Percy flapped onto the chief's front and affectionately pecked crumbs out of his beard.

"We've tried everything to wake him," said Erik. "Sang rude songs, shouted insults in his ear – Olaf even did a big smelly burp right in his face, but nothing has worked." He gazed down at Harald sadly.

Out of the shadows stepped the wiry figure of Ragwich. The soothsayer thrust out his arms and roared.

"OOGAH-GEEGAH!"

Erik gasped. "He's receiving a prophecy!"

Ragwich launched into a series of wild jerky poses, his chicken headdress flapping in such a way that it seemed to be copying his moves.

An awestruck hush fell over everyone in the hall. Everyone except Velda, who turned her nose up and folded her arms. "I've seen cow pats with better acting skills than that!"

And Thorfinn, who seemed to think Ragwich was doing some sort of dance. He began clapping along and tapping his foot. "A very jolly jig, my friend. Keep going!"

Oh, and Oswald, who was picking his nose.

"GOOGAH-GOOGAH!" Ragwich thrust one arm in the air, then brought it down slowly to level an accusing finger at Thorfinn and his friends. "Those three! THEYYYY are to blame for this! THEYYYY disrespected the gods!"

"I'll do more than that in a minute!" snarled Velda, dancing about like a boxer and swinging her fists.

"THEYYYY must be BANISHED from this village,"
roared the soothsayer. "FOR EVER!" He turned to
Erik and slowly twirled his sparkly medallion.

Erik's face went oddly blank. "BANISHED..."
he repeated, his one eye spinning strangely.
"FOR EVER."

Ragwich's medallion glinted in the firelight.

"YOU are Harald's second-in-command, are you
not?"

Erik nodded absently.

"Which means YOU are in charge now."

"I AM IN CHARGE," Erik said slowly.

"Don't you dare listen to him, Ear-Masher!" cried
Velda, twirling her axe.

When Erik turned to face them, his eye was glazed, but he was roaring at the top of his voice: "GET OUT! BE GONE! You are BANISHED from this village!"

Swords raised, Erik's men lunged towards Thorfinn and his friends.

CHAPTER 6

Harek, who'd been waiting outside, burst through the door of the Great Hall, flattening several of Erik's men by accident. "RUN!" He swung Oswald onto his back, then scooped Thorfinn and Velda up under each arm, Percy flying alongside.

Harek barged his way out of the Great Hall, while Velda squirmed. "HEYYY! This was just about to get interesting!"

Before they knew it, other villagers had joined in the chase, shouting and jeering: "We'll show you for ruining our meaty feast!"

"Yeah, no one wants a polite, scone-baking Viking here!" cried Olaf.

Harek raced across the marketplace in the direction of the fjord. He sprinted from the crowd and tripped, rather than leapt, aboard a waiting longship.

And not just any old longship. Thorfinn gazed up at the coppery green dragon masthead. "Ah, hello old girl!"

The *Green Dragon* was Thorfinn's ship, and his crew was onboard. Thorfinn saluted them. "Hello, my dear old pals!"

"How come you lot are here?" asked Velda.

A warty woman with slimy hair cackled from the back of the boat. This was not in fact a witch who had stowed away on board, but Thorfinn's cook, Gertrude the Grotty. Not that she 'cooked' anything you could actually eat. Her favourite ingredients were insects, some of which were constantly in orbit around her head. "Tee hee! We heards the moose honk!"

"So we guessed Thorfinn would be in trouble," added Grut the Goat-Gobbler, a rotund man who never stopped eating, talking about eating, or indeed thinking about eating. "Is it time for supper yet?" he added. "Being in mortal peril makes me peckish."

Velda leapt straight into action. "No time for that! Cast off, pigdogs!"

"I have an idea! Why don't we go on a little holibobs to France?!" boomed Torsten the Ship-Sinker. Torsten was Thorfinn's navigator. Unfortunately, he wasn't very good with directions. Or ships. "France is THATAWAY!" he added, pointing in the direction of the North Pole.

They pushed the ship away from the bank, and just in time, as a horde of angry villagers led by Olaf and Erik followed behind them, their arms full of Thorfinn's tea party treats.

"GO!" Olaf shouted, launching the food at the escaping ship. "And take your teeny-tiny sandwiches with you!"

CHAPTER 7

Thorfinn and his crew watched as the booing villagers, and the village of Indgar itself, shrank into the distance.

"We're officially homeless!" moaned Grimm the Grim, the final member of Thorfinn's crew and probably the saddest man in the entire Viking world. Everything about him was miserable; even his moustache was droopy.

"My dear, poor dad," said Thorfinn. "I do hope someone will look after him." He absently turned over a small, empty glass bottle in his hands.

"What's that?" asked Velda.

"Oh, I picked it up from the floor of the Great Hall."

Velda gasped. "That's the bottle I saw Ragwich take out of his saddlebag and stuff in his pocket."

"Let me see," warbled Oswald.

The old man pulled out the cork and sniffed the bottle. His eyes nearly popped out of his head. "I thought so. It's a potion of some sort."

Velda snatched the bottle and took a whiff.

Her face turned green. "YUCK! It smells like whale puke!"

"Some kind of sleeping potion, no doubt," Oswald said. "Well spotted, you two. Ragwich must have slipped it into the chief's mead."

"We were right. He *is* a con man. We need to tell Erik the Ear-Masher!" cried Velda.

"I'm afraid he won't listen," sighed Oswald. "He's been hypnotised."

"YOU WHAT?" Velda croaked.

"Didn't you see Erik's eye? Ragwich used that medallion of his."

Thorfinn frowned. "Poison Father? Hypnotise Erik? Whatever for?"

"Because Erik will do whatever Ragwich wants,"

whined Oswald. "Which means the village belongs to Ragwich now."

Velda growled. "And with us banished, he has no one asking awkward questions!"

A wail went up behind them. It was Grimm again, sounding like a seal with toothache. "Being banished is SOOOO depressing!"

Thorfinn fed Percy some crumbs, mulling over their options. His first thought was to seek help from his family, but that would be difficult. His mum was in Iceland running a health spa, having gone into business with Velda's dad, Gunga. And his three brothers were away doing Vikingy things of their own: Wilfred the Spleen-Mincer was invading Poland, Sven the Head-Crusher was captaining the belching team at the Viking Olympics, and Hagar the Brain-Eater was wrestling snakes in Africa. It was up to Thorfinn to save his dad and the village.

Then he had a thought. "Perhaps... if there's a potion to send someone to sleep, there's also a potion that will wake them up again."

"That's it, Thorfinn!" bleated Oswald. He delved inside his robe and pulled out a gigantic map roll, showing the northern sea and the island of Britain. He spread it out across the top of a barrel and squinted at it. "Now..."

"Pardon me, old friend, but what are you doing?" asked Thorfinn.

"You are right, Thorfinn," replied Oswald, pointing at the map. "We are going to need a new potion, one powerful enough to wake up the chief."

"So where do we get one?" asked Velda.

"There's only one potion-maker in the whole Viking world who can make such a thing. And he happens to be my brother."

CHAPTER 8

Velda slapped the old man's back, nearly knocking out his few remaining teeth. "I didn't know you had a brother, Oswald!"

Thorfinn smiled. "I would be delighted to make his acquaintance. But where is he?"

Oswald leaned so close to the map he was practically wiping his nose on it. "That's the problem. He's a long way off." He jabbed his bony finger at a spot on the western coast of Britain. "Piebald lives here, in the Kingdom of Galloway."

Thorfinn licked his forefinger and held it in the air.

"Well, there's a fair wind."

"Then what are we waiting for?" Velda pointed the crew in the direction of the setting sun. "Get rowing, you stinking clowns!"

They pulled hard on their oars, breaking into song, as Vikings always did when they set out on their voyages to rob unsuspecting villages of all their worldly goods.

"OH, OH, OH, OH,
THE VIKINGS WILL A-ROVING GO.
AY, AY, AY, AY,
OUR ENEMIES WILL RUN AWAY.
UM, UM, UM, UM,
WE'LL STEAL YOUR GOLD AND KICK YOUR BUM!"

The journey across the North Sea to Britain took twice as long as it should have. Mainly because Torsten went east when he should have been going west, and north when he should have been going south.

Things got worse when the food ran out. Grut ran around like a maniac, pleading frantically, "Has anyone got any chicken? Sausages? Those little cubes of cheese they give out at parties?" However, the crew's mood improved slightly when Gertrude declared that she'd also run out of insects.

Days passed. As they sailed down the Scottish coast, Thorfinn and Oswald watched the waves from the bow. "Why have you never spoken of your brother?" asked Thorfinn.

"Piebald and I haven't talked in thirty years," replied Oswald.

"Why ever not, old bean?"

"We fell out," he said simply.

"Oh great!" chipped in Velda. "So we don't even know if he's still alive! This could be a wild goose chase."

Oswald pointed out the low-lying coastline in the distance, stretching into the east. "We'll soon find out. That's the Kingdom of Galloway."

Peering through his telescope, Thorfinn spied a village clustered around a wide, sheltered bay. "And that looks like the perfect place to go ashore."

CHAPTER 9

The *Green Dragon* landed at a village made up of whitewashed cottages with thatched roofs. At its heart stood a large church.

"If I'm not mistaken," whined Oswald, "this is the village of Whithorn."

"Is it friendly?" asked Velda.

"Friendly enough, I should think. The people are part-Viking."

As they tied up on the pier, a squat man who they took to be the local sheriff came marching towards them. His face was anything BUT friendly.

"Who are you lot?!" he growled.

"Friendly?!" snorted Velda, raising her axe. "I feel about as welcome as elk vomit in a bathing pool."

Thorfinn stepped forward and doffed his helmet. "Pardon me, sir. We're looking for a man named Piebald. He's a potion-maker."

The sheriff gave a deep groan, his whole body sagging. "Aw, not him!"

"So he's alive, then?" asked Oswald.

"He's alive, alright, though it's a miracle I am!" The man flicked his earlobes with his fingers, earlobes which were strangely long and saggy. So long and saggy that they rested on his shoulders.

"Mmm... pork chops," said Grut dreamily, his stomach rumbling loudly as he eyed the man's ears.

"Piebald is how I got these lugs," continued the sheriff. "Him and his stupid potions! I only went to him with an ingrown toenail, and this is what I left with!"

Seeing Thorfinn's kind eyes, the man slumped down on a barrel and sniffed. "It's hard being a sheriff and looking like this. Everyone laughs at me – I've got no authority!"

Thorfinn patted him gently on the shoulder. "There, there. I think you're very sheriff-y."

Meanwhile, Velda shot a fiery glare at Oswald. "I thought you said your brother was the world's best potion-maker?"

Oswald shrugged. "He is... when he wants to be."

"Oh, that bodes well – NOT!"

Thorfinn offered the sheriff a handkerchief,
which the man gratefully took. He blew his nose
loudly, which set his ears wobbling. "Thank you,
young man. It's not every day people are so kind."

Thorfinn gave a polite bow.

The sheriff dried his eyes. "I'd steer well clear of Piebald if I were you. But if you really must go, his clinic is just over the hill, in a small hamlet called Duntroddin."

Velda nodded. "We'll take Grut. He can carry Oswald and his bunions. The rest can stay here."

With a weary grunt, Grut hoisted Oswald onto his back, and they set off over the hill.

Gertrude toddled after them. "Wait for me!"

"No, stay here, Gertrude!" Velda called.

"I wants the potion man to look at my warts," Gertrude explained.

"You want him to cure your warts?"

"NO!" Gertrude replied, insulted. "One of my warts disappeared. I wants him to find it and brings it back."

CHAPTER 10

"Seems like a busy little place, doesn't it?" said Thorfinn cheerfully as they strode into the square at Duntroddin.

One building, larger than the others, had a sign hanging outside:

A steady stream of people were coming and going, and a queue had formed at the door. One man had a hatchet lodged in his head, although he seemed strangely calm about it. A woman behind him was itching all over, as if she was being attacked by killer ants. The man at the end was standing rather stiffly, holding the small of his back and wincing with pain every time he sneezed, which was every five seconds.

"ACHOO! OW... ACHOO! OW..."

Suddenly, another man came staggering out of the doorway, screaming. His right leg was in a splint, and he was waving his arms in the air. But the main cause of his alarm seemed to be the steam that was whistling out of his ears. **"AAARGH!"** he cried, lurching off across the square.

An old man followed him out. He was tall and skinny, with rosy cheeks, and was wearing a long white robe and druid's hood.

"Where are you going? We're not finished!" The old man glanced into the clay beaker he was holding, then back towards the fleeing patient. He burst out in side-splitting laughter. "HAHAHA! GOTCHA!"

Tossing the beaker away, he slapped his hands together and turned to the queue. "Right, who's next?"

The waiting patients glanced at one another in terror, before running in the other direction. The sneezing man with the sore back limped off at surprising speed, yelping,

"ACHOO! OW... ACHOO! OW..."

"Spoilsports!" the old man shouted after them. Then he spotted Thorfinn and his friends. His eyes widened with surprise when he saw Oswald. "I don't believe it, my big brother!"

"Piebald," Oswald said warily.

"Goodness me! How long has it been? Come on, greet your brother properly!" Piebald offered his hand. Oswald eyed him suspiciously for a moment, before grasping it.

"EEEK!" Oswald squeaked and jumped in

the air. He looked at his palm, where a small green frog stared up at him, unimpressed.

Piebald pointed at Oswald and laughed.

"HAHAHA! GOTCHA! Same old Oswald, always falling for it."

Oswald let the frog hop off his hand. Then he wiped the slime on his robe and turned to Thorfinn, rolling his eyes. "I should probably have mentioned this before, but as well as being a famous potion-maker, Piebald is also one of the Viking world's biggest practical jokers."

"What a jolly chap he is," said Thorfinn, stepping forward and shaking Piebald's hand. "Delighted to meet you, sir." Percy, perched on Thorfinn's shoulder, lifted his wing in greeting.

Velda glowered at Piebald. "Don't try any of your stupid tricks on me, Grandad."

Piebald screwed his face up and wiggled his head from side to side. "Ooh-hoo-hoo-hoo-hoo, aren't you a little pocket full of sunshine!"

"Pardon me, sir, but we've come to seek your help," said Thorfinn.

"Well, all my patients have run off, so you may as well come in." Piebald smiled and showed them inside.

"Nice trick with the frog," said Grut, offering up his palm. "Any chance you could magic up a chicken or something? I'm starving."

CHAPTER 11

In the murky interior, the walls were lined with shelves, which were stacked high with jars and pots, all filled with different-coloured ingredients.

One end of the clinic was taken up with sick beds and workbenches. At the other end stood a massive bookcase and a large copper mixing vat.

"Please, sit," said Piebald. He turned away for a moment while they perched around a table. "Here, let's have some tea." Piebald brought over a tray of beakers. He offered Gertrude some honey from a little pot. "Would you like to sweeten your tea, dear?"

She shook her head. "No thanks, but I will takes the dead wasp that's stuck in there." She poked her finger in and hooked out the wasp's corpse. "Mmmmm, crunchy!"

Piebald settled down next to Thorfinn and raised his beaker. "To long-lost family!"

They drank in silence, but Piebald seemed to be

struggling to stifle a giggle.

"I'm feeling a bit weird," Grut said, as a mass of hair suddenly started sprouting from his face, neck and the backs of his hands. In seconds, he had transformed into something resembling a huge ball of fur. Even his eyes had disappeared under the thick hair. "Hey! Who turned out the lights?" he cried.

"Piebald! You didn't!" shouted Oswald.

Piebald nodded, his face brimming with glee. "I did! I did!"

"He did what?" snapped Velda.

"He slipped some kind of potion in the tea." Oswald stared down into his beaker.

"His is called *Bushy Burden.*" Piebald nodded at some labelled bottles above the workbench, then turned to Gertrude. "And yours is *Frump's Flip.*"

"I dont's feel any different," Gertrude shrieked. Except she LOOKED different. Her warts had disappeared, and her hair, always lank and greasy, was now arranged in a sleek beehive hairdo. Even the flies that constantly circled her head flew off. "Hey, guyz, wheres you going?" she called after them.

Thorfinn held up a small mirror for her. Anyone else might have been pleased with their new look, but Gertrude screeched in horror. "Aiee! I is orribles!"

As for Oswald, his face went pale, then he leaned to one side and let loose a giant ripping FART.

PAAAAAAAARP!

"Oh, dear!" he said simply, finding himself engulfed

in multi-coloured gas that rose from his bottom.

"HAHAHA! GOTCHA!" Piebald bounced with joy. "*Pumping Posset* – a potion that gives you rainbow farts! I mean, what's not to like?"

In the commotion, Percy nudged Thorfinn towards Velda. Her face was changing. Her fiery eyes suddenly became pleasant and warm. Her sullen frown turned into a sunny smile. And it wasn't just her face... She dropped her axe, stood up perfectly straight and clasped her hands together primly. "Goodness me!" she said, in a polite voice as she looked down at herself. "Why am I dressed like an unwashed ruffian?"

"Velda?" Thorfinn stared.

"Yes, my dear fellow?" she replied pleasantly.

"HAHAHA! GOTCHA!" cried Piebald. "She had

a dose of *Toerag's Twist*. That's what she gets for being rude." Piebald nodded at Thorfinn. "Now it's your turn. Your potion's called *Bunny's Bane*."

Thorfinn gave him a big friendly smile. "Pardon me, my dear sir, but I'm afraid you're mistaken. You see, I spotted you putting potion in the beakers, so I swapped your tea with mine."

Piebald gaped in shock. "You mean *I* got the *Bunny's Bane?*"

Thorfinn nodded, leaning towards him and asking eagerly, "Did I do a good joke?"

Now it was Oswald's turn to burst out laughing. "Ha! For once, you're the one who's been GOTCHA'd, Piebald!"

A look of confusion flashed across Piebald's face as his front teeth began to lengthen. His nose twitched, his ears wiggled, and he started making a rabbity nibbling sound.

"Carrots! I must have c-c-c-carrots!" Piebald leapt off his stool and hopped out the door.

"Dear me," said Velda mildly. "That poor gentleman believes he is a rabbit."

Grut, or rather the big ball of hair that contained Grut, rolled onto the floor, chortling loudly. "Ha! The old goat got what he deserves!"

Oswald, coughing and wafting away his colourful clouds, called to Thorfinn. "We still need his help – you'd better go after him!"

CHAPTER 12

Thorfinn quickly studied the rack nearby and picked out two small bottles. He whistled cheerfully as he tossed one to Oswald. "Here, my good friend. You might want to share it with the others."

He dashed outside to find Piebald crouched down, burrowing a hole in the ground with his hands. A couple of real rabbits sat on the grass nearby, watching with puzzlement.

Thorfinn drummed his fingers on his chin for a moment, before picking a bunch of dock leaves. He dribbled the contents of the bottle he'd taken from

the clinic over the leaves, then wafted them under
the old man's nose. "How about some lovely salad,
nice rabbit?"

Piebald sniffed the leaves, before snatching them
between his teeth and munching them down. "That
should do the trick," said Thorfinn.

Piebald stopped digging. He stared down at his hands, crusted with dirt, then up at Thorfinn, before erupting in a huge belly laugh. "HAHAHA! Brilliant! But how did you know how to cure me?"

Thorfinn showed him the label on the little bottle, which read:

"Fortunately, Oswald taught me how to read Latin. *Antidotum* means antidote – the cure."

Piebald rolled around laughing, slapping his thigh. Then he gave a loud **HICCUP!**

"Sorry, hiccups are one of the side effects from my potions," he explained. "It's the one thing I can't seem to cure. It'll stop eventually."

Velda came skipping over from the clinic, singing happily. "Tra-la laaa..."

"Goodness me." Thorfinn shared a look with Percy, who had just fluttered onto his shoulder. They had never seen Velda skip like that, except over the unconscious bodies of her defeated foes.

Velda gasped with delight and clapped her hands together. "Look! A lovely bunny wabbit!" She snatched up one of the nearby rabbits and squeezed it to her chest. The poor creature's eyes nearly popped out of its head. "Oh, my little bunny-wunny-kins!"

Grut followed behind her, tossing an empty antidote bottle over his shoulder. The hair was falling off him like snow off a roof. "All this moulting is making me hungry."

Behind him, Gertrude shook her beehive hair apart. It was back to its usual lank and greasy state, and the flies returned to buzz around her head. "Hey, welcome back guyz, I missed you." Then she, like Piebald, gave a loud **HICCUP!**

Suddenly, Velda transformed back into her usual self. Her scowl returned, and she looked very much like she wanted to hit someone.

"YUCK! What's this?" She tossed the rabbit into a bush. "And where's my axe?"

Now it was Grut's turn to **HICCUP!** As he did, Velda's face changed *again*. The pleasant expression returned, as did the friendly smile.

Then, a few seconds later, Grut, Piebald and Gertrude all **HICCUPED** together, and back came Velda's fierce and fiery eyes.

"AARGH!" she yelled. "What's happening to me!?"

Oswald stomped over. Thorfinn had never seen him so angry. He was wafting away the last of the rainbow gas cloud, whining at the top of his lungs: **"PIEBAAAAALD! YOU'VE GONE TOO FAR THIS TIME!"**

CHAPTER 13

"See! This is exactly why you and I fell out!" Oswald snapped.

"Hey!" cried Piebald. "It was YOU who fell out with ME!"

"Is it any wonder? You gave me a potion that made me talk gobbledygook for a whole year. Nobody knew what in Odin's name I was talking about!"

Piebald shrugged. "You already talked a load of gobbledygook; no one even noticed the difference." He turned and clapped Thorfinn on the shoulder. "Now, did I mention how much I like this boy?"

"Making someone talk nonsense for a year sounds rather naughty," replied Thorfinn. "But I like you too – you don't mind the joke being on yourself."

"Well, a joke's a joke, isn't it?" Piebald laughed.

"I don't suppose you've noticed," Thorfinn added, "but Velda's potion hasn't quite worn off. Every time someone hiccups, she changes."

"The other potions were quite weak," Piebald explained, a grin spreading across his face. "*Toerag's Twist*, on the other hand, is very strong. She'll be switching between her usual self and her opposite self for seven days."

"Seven days!" Velda snarled and rolled up her sleeves. "Brother or not, Oswald, he's for it!"

Piebald whimpered. "That girl's unhinged. I don't see why I should help you if she's just going to beat me up!"

"Oh, we can fix that." Oswald gave a loud **HICCUP!** and Velda changed back again, just as the rabbit she'd tossed into the bushes came hopping out into the open.

"My bunny wunny!" Velda cried. She scooped it up, squeezing it tight.

The rabbit shot Thorfinn a look of panic. "Don't worry, my furry friend," Thorfinn whispered in its ear. "I'll rescue you if need be."

Oswald went on, "If you don't help us, Piebald, we'll hiccup and bring Velda back. And you REALLY don't want us to do that!"

Piebald sighed. "FINE. What is it you need?"

Oswald lowered himself down onto the grass, which took about ten minutes and involved lots of ooh-ing and oww-ing. He told his brother about Ragwich coming to Indgar, and how the soothsayer had poisoned Harald and hypnotised Erik to take control of the village. "Here's the bottle he used," he said.

Piebald snatched it off him, uncorked it and sniffed. "Oof! That's putrid!"

"Do you know this potion, my prank-loving pal?" asked Thorfinn.

"Yes. It's called *Goodnight Gloop*. A very powerful potion indeed – there's only one cure. The good news is that it's straightforward – a second dose of *Goodnight Gloop*... except with one vitally important added ingredient."

"Which is?" asked Oswald.

"Ah, that's the tricky bit. We'll need to steal a hair from a king's beard."

"Why a king?" Thorfinn asked.

Piebald sat chewing his gums for a moment, before spitting out some mushed-up dock leaf left over from earlier. "Royal hair has special curing properties when brewed properly," he explained. "We could use hair from a queen, but bearded lady rulers are rather rare in these parts, unfortunately."

Oswald pondered this. "Where's the nearest royal?"

"That's King Fergus of Galloway," replied Piebald. "His seat is at Threave, several days' march along the coast."

"Thank my lucky bunions we have a ship that can take us there," said Oswald.

"We must go, right away," said Thorfinn. "My dear old dad is depending on us."

Piebald sucked his teeth loudly. "Just so you know – I'm not the most popular person at King Fergus's court."

"I wonder why," sighed Oswald.

"It's not my fault people don't have a sense of humour," sniffed Piebald. "Anyway, I'm sure the king has forgotten about our little... misunderstanding."

"I'm sure he has," smiled Thorfinn politely. "Let's get going, dear pals." He helped Oswald to his feet, which looked and sounded like the crew hoisting the mast on the *Green Dragon*.

Gertrude halted suddenly and began to give a loud **HIC —** but Oswald snapped his hand over her mouth just in time, as Velda came skipping over in their direction.

"Tra-la-LAAAA! Are we going?" she asked. "Oh GOODIE! An adventure! How delightful!"

CHAPTER 14

Back on the longship, Velda, or 'Not-Velda' as they now called her, hummed happily as she made herself a dress out of an old sail. Then she ripped the flaps off a wicker basket and fashioned them into a pair of fairy wings, which she strapped to her back. To cap it all off she made a wand out of a birch twig and the head of a thistle she'd collected on the walk back to the ship. "LAH-DEE-DAAAHH!"

Gracefully, she stepped up onto a barrel, waving her wand and pinching the end of her dress with her fingertips. "I say, would you be so good as to cast off for me, *purr-lease?*"

The crew looked round at one other, confused, while Thorfinn bowed his head at her. "What admirable politeness, dear pal."

Not-Velda curtsied back. "But of course, my good sir."

They sailed out of the bay. Torsten turned them west, towards the Atlantic Ocean, before Thorfinn gently steered them back east, along the coastline of Galloway. After rounding another headland, they took to the oars, rowing the longship up a river until they could go no further. The rest of the journey would have to be on foot.

"We'd better take Harek with us, in case the king tries to kill us on sight," said Oswald, glaring at Piebald.

Leaving the others behind with the boat, the group

marched on (apart from Not-Velda, who skipped), making camp just as the sun was going down.

Later, as they sat round the campfire eating stew, Piebald unlocked a leather case he'd brought along. He flipped open the top and folded out the sides to reveal a miniature potion-making laboratory. Then he used a pocket knife to chop up ingredients before tossing them all together and heating the mixture over the fire. Beads of sweat appeared on his brow as he stirred, a magnifying glass held to one eye.

"Here it is!" he said finally, pouring a green bubbling mixture into a small bottle. "*Goodnight Gloop*: the potion the soothsayer used on your chief."

Oswald nosed the bottle. "Yuck! Yes, that's the same stinky potion alright."

"Now all we need to do is steal a hair from King Fergus's beard," said Piebald.

"Pardon me, friends," said Thorfinn. "But could we not just politely *ask* the king for a hair? Stealing is wrong."

"But then the potion won't work," replied Piebald. "It HAS to be stolen, pinched, snaffled, pilfered!"

"We're Vikings, stealing is what we do!" chipped in Harek, as he ladled some hot stew into his own lap.

"ARRGGHH!"

"And it's the only way to wake your father and save the village," droned Oswald.

Thorfinn's brow furrowed, then he shook his head firmly. "I want to save my poor father, but stealing isn't right."

Oswald sighed and rubbed his hand across his face. "Then I'm afraid we're rather stuck. Ugh! We need Velda back. She would know what to do."

They gazed over at Not-Velda, who was sitting under a tree playing tea parties with the rabbit she'd smuggled from Duntroddin. It looked furious, not least because she'd named it Mr Fluffikins.

"NO!" yelled Piebald. "I prefer her as she is now –
SAFE!"

Oswald groaned and scratched his head. "It's
been a long day. Let's sleep on it and see if we can
find a solution tomorrow."

CHAPTER 15

As they stamped out their fire the next morning, Piebald declared that he had found an answer to their conundrum, but he wouldn't tell anyone what it was. "You'll just have to trust me."

They forged on, across fields and over hills, until at last they came to a large, forbidding wooden fort. It stood on an island in the middle of a river. "That's Threave, the king's castle," announced Piebald.

"Will he see you?" Oswald asked.

"Maybe," his brother replied. "Either that or he'll decorate his throne room with our heads."

"Supposing he does agree to see us," added Harek. "How are we supposed to steal a hair from his beard? He'll have soldiers protecting him. And how do we escape? I can't carry all of you."

Thorfinn patted Piebald on the back. "I'm sure dear Piebald here has thought of that."

The potion-maker smiled weakly.

They walked over the drawbridge and Piebald stopped in front of the guards, giving a polite cough.

He hadn't even spoken before one guard cried out, "YOU!" He grabbed Piebald by the scruff of his neck and hauled him through the gate. "Straight to the king with you, you scoundrel!"

"This bodes well," muttered Oswald with a sigh.

"At least we're going to see the king," said Thorfinn.

"The king?" cried Not-Velda. "Oh how jolly spiffing!"

In the centre of the fort stood a large roundhouse with a thatched roof. The guards dragged them inside.

"And you are?" asked the king, eyeing them wearily from his throne. He was a short, stubby man with a trim beard, sitting in a shaft of light cast down from a chimney hole in the roof. One side of his mouth was swollen, and he was cradling it carefully.

Thorfinn stepped forward and doffed his helmet. "Good day to you, dear king. It's an honour to—"

The guards pushed past him, throwing Piebald

to the floor before leaving with a threatening glare.

The king's face flushed as he eyed the old man.

"YOU! You haf some cheek coming back here. Fanks

to you and your awful potion I waf fneezing Bruffelf fproutf and roaft potatoeff for free whole dayf!"

Piebald chuckled. "*Yuletide Yuck*! It's a classic!"

"And now," continued King Fergus, "I've got fif awful toofache." He clutched his mouth and moaned.

"Ooh, I can help with that," said Piebald.

"Can you?" the king asked suspiciously. "Or if it anofer trick?"

"Er, not at all. That's why I'm here. To give you the cure for your toothache. Isn't that right, friends?" Piebald glanced round at Thorfinn and the others. Thorfinn gave a well-meaning smile, Percy ruffled his feathers awkwardly, and Harek's eyes shifted about from side to side, though sadly not at the same time. Oswald, however, was glaring at his brother furiously. Not-Velda was too busy to notice, making matching crowns for herself and Mr Fluffikins with some flowers she'd picked outside.

Piebald turned to a side table where a goblet and jug had been set out. He poured something into the cup before presenting it to the king. "Here you go, your royalness."

The king looked at the goblet, then at Piebald, then at the others. He grimaced and clutched his jaw. "OUCH! Okay, anyfing to ftop fif pain!"

He snatched the potion and supped it. His face screwed up. "Euch! Fhat's PUTRID!" Suddenly, his eyes drooped and he slumped forward, rolling onto the floor with a CRUMP. A long, droning snore erupted from his nose.

ZZZZZZZZZZ...

Piebald laughed. "HAHAHA! A ROYAL GOTCHA!"

"You didn't!" cried Oswald. "Tell me you didn't just give *Goodnight Gloop* to the king?!"

"I did!" he replied gleefully. "I solved your problem. Now you'll *have* to steal one of his whiskers in order to wake him up again."

"Oh dear," said Thorfinn, who knelt down to tuck a cushion under the king's head. "That's very clever, my friend. Sneaky, but clever."

Percy fluttered onto the king, eyeing up his beard. He was just about to peck out a hair, but was thwarted by two guards bursting into the hall, followed by a sergeant-at-arms. They spotted King

Fergus lying slumped on the floor, a guilty-looking pigeon perched on his chest.

"Arrest them!" barked the sergeant.

"Ah..." said Piebald. "I didn't think of that."

CHAPTER 16

A steady **drip-drip** of water echoed somewhere in the darkness of the castle dungeon. Thorfinn gazed pleasantly out of the tiny barred window. "At least we have a nice view."

"Of the gallows, Thorfinn," said Oswald, his head in his hands. Outside, the hangman was busy stringing up rope ready for his next victims. "That's for us, you know."

In the corner, Not-Velda was putting the final touches to her flower crown (Mr Fluffikins had already eaten his). She finished, then placed it on top of her head. "Ta-daaaa! Good day, your majesty!" She bowed at Harek.

The large man gazed around uncertainly, before clumsily bowing back. "And, er, good day to you, er... Not-Velda."

"The good news is that I may have a plan for removing a whisker from the king's beard," said Thorfinn, stroking Percy's speckled brow. "If only we can escape from here first."

"In that case, we definitely need Velda back," whined Oswald.

Piebald waved his hands frantically. "NO! We're in an enclosed space."

"We're in a scrape, brother, and Velda is good in a scrape," replied Oswald. "Now please excuse me, but there's something I've been dying to do for days."

"It's not another multi-coloured bottom burp, is it?" asked Harek.

Oswald took a deep breath and...

HICCUP!

Velda stopped singing. She stared down at her fairy costume in horror. "EURGH!" Clawing off her crown, she threw it on the floor and stamped on it, shouting, "I. AM. A. VIKING!" Then she tore off her fairy wings and flung her wand onto the pile. "Anyone got a match?"

"Afraid not, old friend," said Thorfinn. "We were actually wondering if you could lend a hand."

Velda leaned against a pillar and folded her arms. "Sure, what's the beef?"

Thorfinn explained. Velda nodded, then jabbed her finger at Piebald. "Okay, first of all, when we get out of here, I'm going to toss him in the nearest river."

"You have NO sense of humour!" protested Piebald.

"Oh, shut up!" snapped Oswald. "It's the least you deserve!"

Velda picked up the rackety old metal tray that their dinner slops had been brought in on, then tossed it against the wall. The tray clattered loudly, scattering plates and bowls across the stone floor. Then she sighed and reluctantly pulled her fairy costume back on.

"Might this be part of an escape plan?" asked Thorfinn.

"'Fraid so," Velda grumbled, just as the guard came stomping up the corridor carrying a flaming torch.

"Now someone hiccup," Velda instructed.

Oswald shrugged his shoulders. "Sorry, I'm all out."

"Ooh, may I have a go?" said Thorfinn. He took a huge gulp of air, held up his forefinger and waited. A moment later, he produced a gentle, ever-so-polite **HICCUP!** "Pardon me!" he giggled.

"What's all this racket?" barked the guard. His face appeared through the bars, cruel and battle-scarred. He eyed the prisoners with disgust, until he saw Velda. Gentle, polite Velda, wearing fairy wings and an angelic look on her face.

She opened her mouth and sang, in a lovely, clear voice that filled the dungeon's dismal depths.

Oh, oh, oh, oh,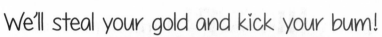

The Vikings will a-roving go.

Ay, ay, ay, ay,

Our enemies will run away.

Um, um, um, um,

We'll steal your gold and kick your bum!

"Awww!" The guard melted. He leant down to smile at Not-Velda. "What a little angel!"

Just then, Harek's giant hand reached out, grabbed the guard's head and WHACKED it against the metal bars.

D-OINNNGGG!

The man slumped to the floor. Not-Velda reached through the bars and plucked the keys off his belt.

"Ooh, look! Sparkly!"

CHAPTER 17

Thorfinn led his friends up the steps out of the cold dungeon. They weaved through corridors, ducking every so often to stay out of sight of the guards.

As they passed through the courtyard, the king's roundhouse was in view, but the sound of heavy footsteps approached around the corner. Thorfinn swiftly spied an open door and ushered them all inside. They found themselves squashed inside a cramped room, which looked and smelled, like a...

"URGH! Toilet!" said Velda, who was now back to her usual self thanks to a well-timed hiccup from

Harek. "It stinks worse than an elk's armpit in here."

Percy covered his beak with his wing.

"Do you think this is the king's other throne?" asked Harek, peering at the toilet and almost falling in headfirst.

"Cork it!" hissed Velda. "We don't have much time." She flicked the thistly tip off Not-Velda's wand, then passed it to Thorfinn.

"Thank you, dear friend." Thorfinn knelt down, using the twig to draw a map of the roundhouse on the sawdust-covered floor. "Poor King Fergus is lying in the middle of the roundhouse, here. There's only one door, at the front, and there are two guards inside. So we'll have to use the only other way in – the chimney hole in the roof."

Velda patted a coil of rope around her chest that she'd stolen from the hangman. "I'll lower Thorfinn down, then Percy will swoop in and pluck the hair. Thorfinn will add it to the potion and give it to the king."

Percy puffed up his chest and raised a wing in salute.

"What will I do?" asked Harek.

"Something that doesn't involve a lot of hand – eye coordination," growled Velda.

"It's been a long time since I climbed anything," Oswald wheezed, sounding like a deflating set of bagpipes.

"Me too," added Piebald.

"Don't worry," Velda smirked. "I've got another job for you two."

Outside, Harek went off to 'borrow' a cart for their escape while Thorfinn and Velda sneaked around the back of the king's roundhouse. They propped an abandoned ladder against the roof and climbed.

Slowly, they crept across the thatch to the

chimney hole, where they peered inside. King Fergus was lying on a table down below, snoozing peacefully. Two guards stood to attention, facing towards the door.

Thorfinn tied the rope around his waist then handed the rest to Velda. "My dear friend, would you please be so good as to lower me down?"

Velda spat in her hands, then grabbed hold of the rope, stretching it round her shoulders and digging in her heels to take Thorfinn's weight. "No probs. Ready when you are."

CHAPTER 18

Piebald burst through the roundhouse door, leaning on his brother and wailing like the ghost of an elderly lady with no teeth. Wearing their hoods up as a basic disguise, the two old men staggered towards the guards.

"Help!" cried Piebald. He held his hands up to them. The thumb of one hand was bent under his fingers, and the thumb of the other hand was half-hidden behind his forefinger. He kept moving them together, then apart, over and over, which made it look as if the top of his thumb had been chopped off. "I've been de-thumbed!" he wailed. The illusion was helped by a splash of 'blood', which came from a vial of reddish potion Piebald had in his pouch.

Seeing that the brothers were in place, Velda took the chance to lower Thorfinn gently through the chimney hole.

Unfortunately, the guards either didn't buy Piebald's trick or they didn't care that some doddering old man had lost one of his digits. One of them stepped towards the brothers, brandishing his spear. "Be on your way! Go on, you pair of old FARTS!"

"Oh, er..." The two brothers fidgeted and glanced at each other. Their plan was already falling apart.

And it got worse. On the roof, a hungry Mr Fluffikins chose that moment to pop his head out of Velda's pocket and start chewing furiously on the first thing he could find... which just happened to be the rope in Velda's hands. It slipped through her grasp, and Thorfinn dropped like a stone.

WHOOSH!

Velda hung on for dear life and he jolted to a halt just a few feet above King Fergus, his arms and legs spread out like a starfish.

"Oh dear," he whispered.

Velda's face turned red, then purple, as she clutched the rope. One more slip and Thorfinn

would land on top of the conked-out king.

Just as the rope began to slide through Velda's

fingers, a pair of giant hands grabbed it tight.

Harek's face appeared through the chimney, smiling and waving at Thorfinn. "Who's clumsy now!" he grinned, before toppling halfway through the hole and getting wedged in.

Thorfinn held his breath, watching Oswald and Piebald, who were stammering and sweating in front of the two guards.

"Think of something!" Piebald hissed to his brother.

"Me?" Oswald whined back. "Why should I think of something? This is all your fault!"

"Oh, shut it, Noseybonk!"

Oswald spluttered. "How DARE you call me that!" He turned to the guards, their act forgotten. "That was a horrible nickname he made up for me at school."

"Call you what? Noseybonk? NOSEYBONK!

NOSEYBONK!" Piebald did a funny little dance, shouting Oswald's childhood nickname over and over.

"Shut up! SHUT UP!" yelped Oswald, and the two brothers came to blows, standing on their tiptoes and slapping each other's hands. They looked like penguins doing a courtship dance.

The guards gazed in astonishment for a second, before collapsing in hysterical laughter.

Seeing their opportunity, Thorfinn cast a look up at the now dislodged Harek, who nodded and lowered him down the final few inches towards the sleeping king.

Thorfinn reached out his hand towards King Fergus's beard – but it seemed to be getting further away. The rope, tied round Thorfinn's middle, was twirling him – *very* slowly – away from the king's face.

Thorfinn's brow furrowed, before his eyes sparkled with an idea. Calmly, he began to do breaststroke, as if taking a pleasant dip in a tranquil fjord.

Velda and Harek shared a look of disbelief. But Thorfinn's display of mid-air swimming seemed to work, and before long his rope swung him back round towards King Fergus.

Right on cue, Percy swooped down and landed on the king's chest, pulling out a single hair from his beard.

PLUCK!

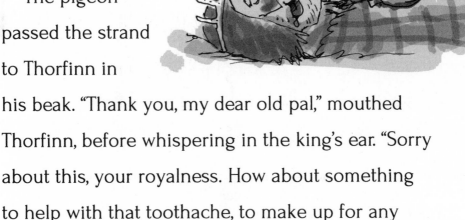

The pigeon passed the strand to Thorfinn in his beak. "Thank you, my dear old pal," mouthed Thorfinn, before whispering in the king's ear. "Sorry about this, your royalness. How about something to help with that toothache, to make up for any inconvenience?" Thorfinn delved into one of his pockets and pulled out a tiny clove, which he gently popped inside the king's swollen cheek.

Meanwhile, Piebald and Oswald had stopped fighting and were now in the middle of a brotherly heart-to-heart. The guards were completely engrossed in the drama, the sleeping king forgotten.

"You were so mean when we were children," sniffed Oswald. "Always playing tricks!"

"Well, you were so serious all the time!" replied Piebald. "All I ever wanted was for you to laugh at one of my jokes."

"But I did!" cried Oswald. "That time you catapulted Granny into the midden, I laughed so hard I threw up my kippers!"

"HA! Did you?!" cried Piebald.

"I did! I did!" droned Oswald, laughing.

"Oh, you don't know how happy that makes me!"

Piebald beamed and put his arm around his brother. "What do you say, shall we put the past behind us?"

"Let's, little brother," replied Oswald. "As long as you promise never to call me Noseybonk ever again?"

"Of course not!" grinned Piebald, crossing his fingers behind his back.

"Aww! I love a happy ending!" blubbed one of the guards. They were both in floods of tears, each using the other's uniform as a handkerchief.

While all this was going on, Thorfinn mixed the hair into the bottle of *Goodnight Gloop*, his tongue sticking out in concentration. Then, wedging a tiny funnel between the king's lips, he poured in some of the putrid potion.

They didn't hang around for the king to awaken. Harek hauled Thorfinn back up, while Oswald and Piebald retreated from the bawling guards, who pulled them in for a group hug as they were leaving.

Together, Thorfinn and his friends jumped into Harek's stolen cart and raced off towards the ship, and home.

CHAPTER 19

The village of Indgar was a much-changed place since Thorfinn and his friends had been banished.

No more roaring! No more fist fights! No more meat! A sad, turnip-scented fog hung over everyone.

The villagers were sitting in the square around the long tables that Thorfinn had used for his tea party. Their heads were bent, and they worked feverishly, peeling mountains of stinky turnips in a production line.

A short distance away, perched above the shore, Ragwich reclined in an open-air bathtub. He hummed idly, twiddling the legs of his giant chicken headdress while a stream of men trooped down from the woods, adding firewood to the flames heating the bathwater.

Erik the Ear-Masher appeared at Ragwich's side, his face still strangely blank. A towel was draped over one arm, and he carried a silver tray with a goblet. "Your elderberry mead."

"Ah, thank you," said Ragwich. He took a long, relaxing sup. "Are my turnip fries done yet?"

Seeing his father bow and shuffle away, Olaf's eyes flashed with fury. He took a deep breath and stepped up to the bath. "Ragwich, why have you moved your horse into our Great Hall?"

"Why not? You weren't using it," replied the soothsayer calmly.

"There's manure all over the place!" yelled Olaf.

"I'm sure dung isn't the worst thing that's been served up in that hall."

"B-B-But—" Olaf stuttered. He was about to retreat, when he glimpsed movement from the corner of his eye: familiar figures that somehow gave him courage. "And our chief, Harald. You moved him into the grain store." Olaf glanced at the hut that housed both the year's harvest and a giant snoring Viking. The doors were usually locked, but from this angle they looked to be ever-so-slightly open.

"It's got nothing to do with me. Your father is in charge now," said Ragwich, and he smiled, a slippery, snakey smile.

Olaf gestured at the production lines of villagers. "Our people, you've put them to work ten hours a day peeling horrid vegetables."

Ragwich shrugged and sipped his mead.

"And worst of all," Olaf huffed, pointing towards the village cooks, who were stirring boiling cauldrons in the marketplace, "You're forcing us all to eat TURNIP SOUP!"

"I told you, turnips are the food of the gods! Now

off you go, little boy. You're ruining my ME-time."

Olaf trudged off. Ragwich gave a long, satisfied sigh and gazed out at the fjord as he supped his mead. A contented smile spread across his face as he closed his eyes. "Ahhh, peace."

Such was his feeling of relaxation, Ragwich didn't see the pigeon that landed on the edge of his bathtub and dropped a tiny pellet of poo into the steaming water. Nor did he see a small hand, a girl's hand, as it reached over the lip of the bath and tipped a bottle of liquid into his cup.

CHAPTER 20

Meanwhile, in the grain store, Thorfinn was carefully pouring the remaining *Goodnight Gloop* into the sleeping Harald's mouth. The chief sputtered slightly between snores, before he woke with a...

"BAAAAHHHHHHHH!"

"Dearest Dad!" cried Thorfinn, hugging his father tight. "It's lovely to see you awake again!"

"Thorfinn!" Harald leapt to his feet and picked up his son, twirling him in the air, before looking around with a confused stare. "What happened?

Why I am in the grain store?"

"I can explain everything, Father," said Thorfinn.

"You've had a rather long nap..."

Ragwich took another sip of his mead. He didn't notice the strange taste, but there was something he did notice.

One big, scary, ENORMOUS thing.

The doors of the grain store burst open. Standing there, looking ANGRY and giving him the sort of stare that might make Odin himself do a scared little scream, was Harald the Skull-Splitter, legendary Viking chief.

Asleep no more, Harald growled like a hibernating bear that had been woken up by a loud party in next door's den. His eye twitched fast enough to cause a small hurricane.

At his side was Thorfinn, Percy now perched on his shoulder, while Piebald and Oswald tottered up to meet them, arm in arm. The mast of the *Green Dragon* could be glimpsed in the fjord behind them.

"What potion did you make for Ragwich?" Oswald asked his brother.

"Oh, a good one," chortled Piebald. "A good one."

The rest of Thorfinn's crew followed on behind.

Grut the Goat-Gobbler cried out in terror as he glimpsed the village cooks at work. "TURNIPS! Why are they cooking turnips? Am I in hell?!"

Harek laughed heartily. He was SOOO happy to be home. Then he slipped on some spilled turnip soup...

"AIEEEEE!"

...and crashed to the floor in a gloopy heap.

SPLAT!

Velda popped her head over the lip of Ragwich's bathtub, twirling the empty bottle between her fingers and whistling a tune that Vikings only sang at funerals.

The soothsayer leapt out of the tub and whipped on a cloak, his chicken headdress flapping frantically. He thrust out his arms in a dramatic pose and addressed Harald. "Great chief! The gods have woken you from your slumber!"

"Don't even try it, soothsayer. You're not going to slither out of this one!" barked Harald, moving towards him like a hairy mountain lion stalking a goggly-eyed deer.

Ragwich reached for his medallion, except it wasn't around his neck. Percy flapped down and dropped something shiny into Thorfinn's palm. "Is this what you're looking for, dear sir?" Thorfinn asked.

"A-ah," Ragwich stuttered, finally lost for words.

Thorfinn tossed the necklace in the air. Velda whipped out her axe, screamed and chopped it in two before it hit the ground.

Ragwich whimpered, then suddenly clutched his tummy, which gurgled loudly. "Oh my, I feel... a bit... strange..."

CHAPTER 21

Ragwich's eyes bulged. His arms flapped at his sides. He began to scratch at the ground with his bony feet and his head bobbed back and forth. Then he opened his mouth and shrieked:

CLUUUUUUUCKKKK-CLUCK-CLUCK-CLUCK-CLUCK!

"HA!" Oswald slapped his thigh. "Now he really does look like a chicken. Oh, well done, brother!"

"It's called *Barnyard Boogie*," laughed Piebald.

"It'll make him feel a bit *fowl* for a while, geddit?!"
They watched Ragwich as he scuttled away after the other chickens.

CLUUUUUUUCKKKK-CLUCK-CLUCK-CLUCK-CLUCK!

There came a great clatter from the marketplace, where Grut had started a revolution, overturning the cauldrons of boiling turnips and the long tables, scattering mountains of vegetables in the mud. "Fellow Vikings! BURN YOUR TURNIPS! Follow me! I will lead you to MEAT! ROAST CHICKEN! RIB OF BEEF! THOSE LITTLE JUICY COCKTAIL SAUSAGES THE SIZE OF YOUR PINKIES!"

"MEEEAT!" the villagers roared, stamping up and down on the turnips, then charging off after him.

Erik appeared, the blank look gone from his face, with Olaf alongside him. "Sorry, Chief! He hypnotised me!"

"Forget about it, my friend. I'm just glad to be back!" bellowed Harald, slapping Erik so hard across the shoulders that his eye nearly popped out.

Suddenly, Harald gave a loud **HICCUP!**

All eyes turned to Velda, as a kind, pleasant smile spread over her face. Not-Velda was back. "Hmm... Now, where did I put my Mr Fluffikins?" she said in a gentle voice. She reached into her pocket and pulled out a VERY grumpy-looking bunny.

"Oh dear," said Not-Velda as she took in the

bunny's appearance. On the journey home,
Mr Fluffikins appeared to have undergone a
transformation of his own, complete with tiny horned
helmet and warpaint. The bunny bared his teeth.

"Oh!" Piebald sucked his teeth. "I meant to tell you, it's
been seven days. At sunset, *Toerag's Twist* will become
permanent. You'd better decide which Velda you want
— the polite one, or the HOMICIDAL MANIAC one."

They all looked towards the sun, already half-
disappeared below the horizon.

"Not-Velda doesn't hit me," moaned Grimm the
Grim. "Or call me a pigdog."

"Not-Velda doesn't start fights in empty rooms,"
sighed Harek, who was slowly getting to his feet
and wiping turnip gloop from his face.

"And Not-Velda doesn't spit outs my fine cookin,'" chipped in Gertrude the Grotty.

Harald turned to his son. "Thorfinn, what do you think?"

Thorfinn smiled as the sunlight began to disappear. It took him no time at all to make up his mind. "Velda is my friend, and I wouldn't have her any other way."

He took a deep gulp of air, and then...

HICCUP!

Velda leant down, picked up her axe and swung it over her shoulder. "Phew! Thank Odin for that!" She gazed down at her warrior rabbit and grinned. "Come on, I'll call you Fluff-Spitter!" And off they both swaggered.

"Now," said Harald, lifting Thorfinn onto one shoulder as Percy hopped onto the other. "What do I have to do to get some food around here. I haven't eaten in days!"

"Perhaps a nice scone and some crab and lettuce sandwiches, dear Dad?" replied Thorfinn.

Harald gave a booming laugh. "Sounds delicious!"

Together, Oswald and Piebald watched as the sun finally set over Indgar. "Dear me!" whined Oswald. "I'm glad all that excitement is over. What now?"

Piebald grinned mischievously. "How about a nice cup of tea?"

RICHARD THE
PICTURE-CONQUEROR

DAVID THE
STORY-CHIEF

DAVID MACPHAIL left home at eighteen to travel the world and have adventures. After working as a chicken wrangler, a ghost-tour guide and a waiter on a tropical island, he now has the sensible job of writing about yetis and Vikings. At home in Perthshire, Scotland, he exists on a diet of cream buns and zombie movies.

RICHARD MORGAN was born and raised by goblins on the Yorkshire moors. After running away to New Zealand to play with yachts and paint backgrounds for Disney TV he returned to the UK to write and illustrate children's books. He now lives in Cambridge, England, and has a family of goblins of his own.

PIEBALD'S POTION MAKER

Follow these simple steps to create your very own putrid potion!

1. What's your *last name*? That's the *first part* of your potion name. EASY!

2. What *day* of the month were you born? Find out which word makes up the *second part* of your potion name.

1 – Snit
2 – Jinx
3 – Blight
4 – Bother
5 – Trouble
6 – Blast
7 – Twinge
8 – Woe
9 – Piddle
10 – Flip
11 – Wink
12 – Bane
13 – Pulp
14 – Snipe
15 – Sorrow
16 – Thingummy

17 – Twist
18 – Pang
19 – Boogie
20 – Widdle
21 – Burden
22 – Pump
23 – Ruin
24 – Plague
25 – Wrinkle
26 – Curse
27 – Poop
28 – Spin
29 – Snub
30 – Stitch
31 – Bilge

3. Which *month* were you born? That gives you the *effect* of your potion.

January: Weeping warts
February: Galloping eyebrows
March: Purple wee
April: Transform into a moose
May: Musical farts
June: MOO like a cow
July: Hair like worms
August: Uncontrollable dancing
September: Flaming burps
October: Everything you eat tastes of smelly socks
November: Tremendously itchy bottom
December: Speak in gobbledygook

FOR EXAMPLE: David MacPhail was born on the 22nd of May so his potion is:

MACPHAIL'S PUMP, WHICH GIVES YOU MUSICAL FARTS!

FIND MR FLUFFIKINS

Mr Fluffikins has hopped off! Can you help Not-Velda avoid Piebald's potions and find her little bunny-wunny-kins?

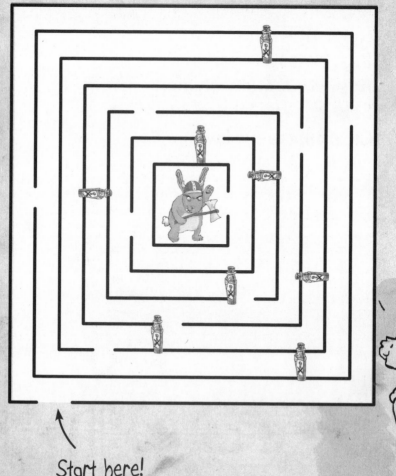

Start here!

RAGWICH'S FOOLPROOF FORTUNE TELLER

Want to predict the future just like Ragwich?
Try his 100 % totally accurate* fortune telling method...

1. Think of a question you want to know the answer to, e.g. "Will it be turnip fries for tea?"

2. Throw a dice...

3. How many dots are on the side facing upwards? (No cheating!)

4. Match it to the key below...

5. WOO-GAH! The gods have spoken – you have your answer!

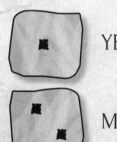 YES

 NO

 MAYBE

 THROW AGAIN!

 ONLY IF IT'S A FULL MOON

 WHO KNOWS?!

*Answers not actually 100 % totally accurate...

PERCY THE PIGEON POST

EST. 799AD   ODINSDAY 18th FEBRUARY   PRICE: ONE FRONT TOOTH

SKULL-SPLITTING NEWS

In what will forever be known as the Awful Invasion the Scots have narrowly missed being invaded by a band of maurauding Vikings, led by the fearsome Chief of Indgar, Harald the Skull-Splitter.

SPORTING HEADLINES

It is the weekend of the annual Gruesome Games. Word on the beach is that Thorfinn and his motley team have to save their village from the clutches of Magnus the Bone-Breaker. Odds are on for a new Chief of Indgar by Monday.

FOULSOME FOOD

It's all about Le Poisson (that's FISH to you boneheads). The King of Norway is on his way to Indgar and he expects a most Disgusting Feast. But there's a poisoner at large and the heat is on in the kitchen...

TORTUROUS TRAVEL

Early booking is essential to visit the Rotten Scots' most famous prisoner (that's Thorfinn) at Castle Red Wolf. Hurry – he may be rescued at any moment!

LOST AND NOT FOUND

A massive hoard of Terrible Treasure stolen from the pesky Scots has mysteriously vanished. Large reward promised for information leading to its recovery.

MISSING PERSONS

The Raging Raiders are prime suspects in the kidnapping of one fed-up, goat-carrying Viking mum. Please report any sightings to Chief Harald the Skull-Splitter.

FIERY FIEND SPOTTED

A Dreadful Dragon was seen above Lerwick's Great Fire Festival. Eyewitness reports of a whooping Thorfinn riding atop the beast's back are yet to be confirmed.

Collect all Thorfinn adventures